ONE TODAY

BY RICHARD BLANCO · ILLUSTRATED BY DAV PILKEY

Ⓛ Ⓑ

Little, Brown and Company
New York   Boston

For Sophia Mei Morera and all the children of our country, and beyond.
May you all be one today and every day through these words.

—RB

To Amy Berkower and Susan Rich for their vision and guidance.

—DP

The illustrations for this book were done in acrylics and India ink. The paintings were photo-graphed for reproduction by John Arnsdorf. The text and display type were set in Hiroshige. This book was edited by Susan Rich and designed by Saho Fujii. The production was supervised by Erika Schwartz, and the production editor was Christine Ma.

ON JANUARY 21, 2013, AT 11:55 AM, in front of an estimated one million people gathered on the National Mall, Barack Obama took the presidential oath and was sworn in to his second term as president of the United States of America.

Moments later, Richard Blanco ascended the podium and read this poem, which he wrote to mark the occasion.

One sun rose on us today, kindled over our shores,
peeking over the Smokies, greeting the faces
of the Great Lakes, spreading a simple truth
across the Great Plains, then charging across the Rockies.

One light, waking up rooftops, under each one, a story
told by our silent gestures moving behind windows.

My face, your face, millions of faces in morning's mirrors,
each one yawning to life, crescendoing into our day:

pencil-yellow school buses, the rhythm of traffic lights,

fruit stands: apples, limes, and oranges arrayed like rainbows

begging our praise.

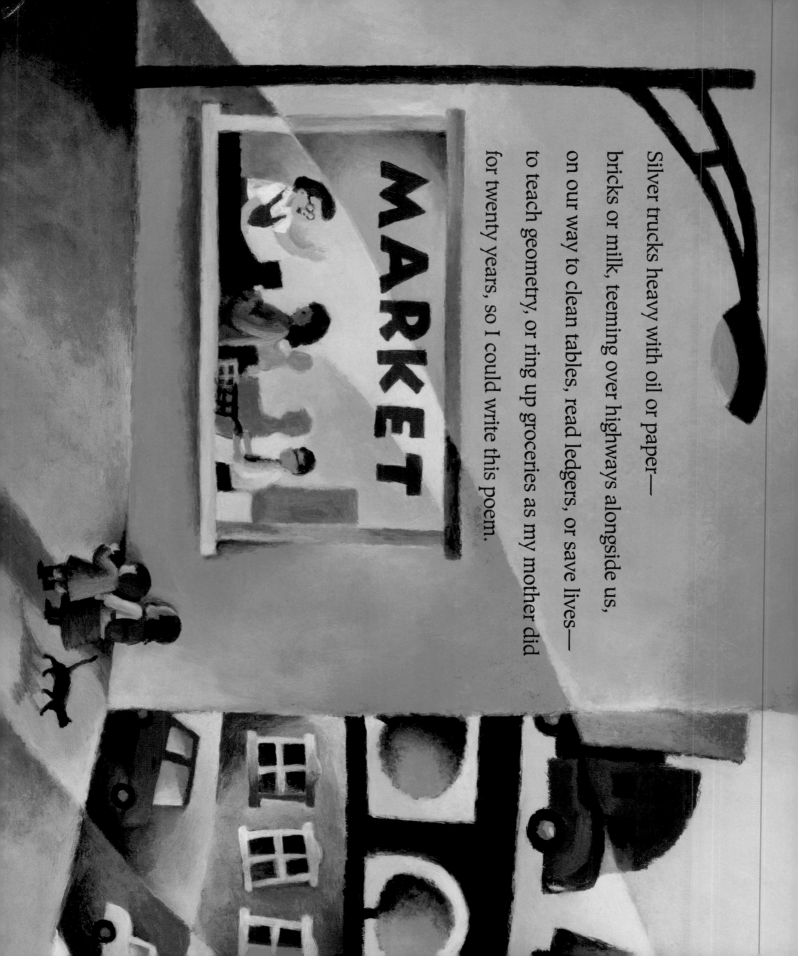

Silver trucks heavy with oil or paper—
bricks or milk, teeming over highways alongside us,
on our way to clean tables, read ledgers, or save lives—
to teach geometry, or ring up groceries as my mother did
for twenty years, so I could write this poem.

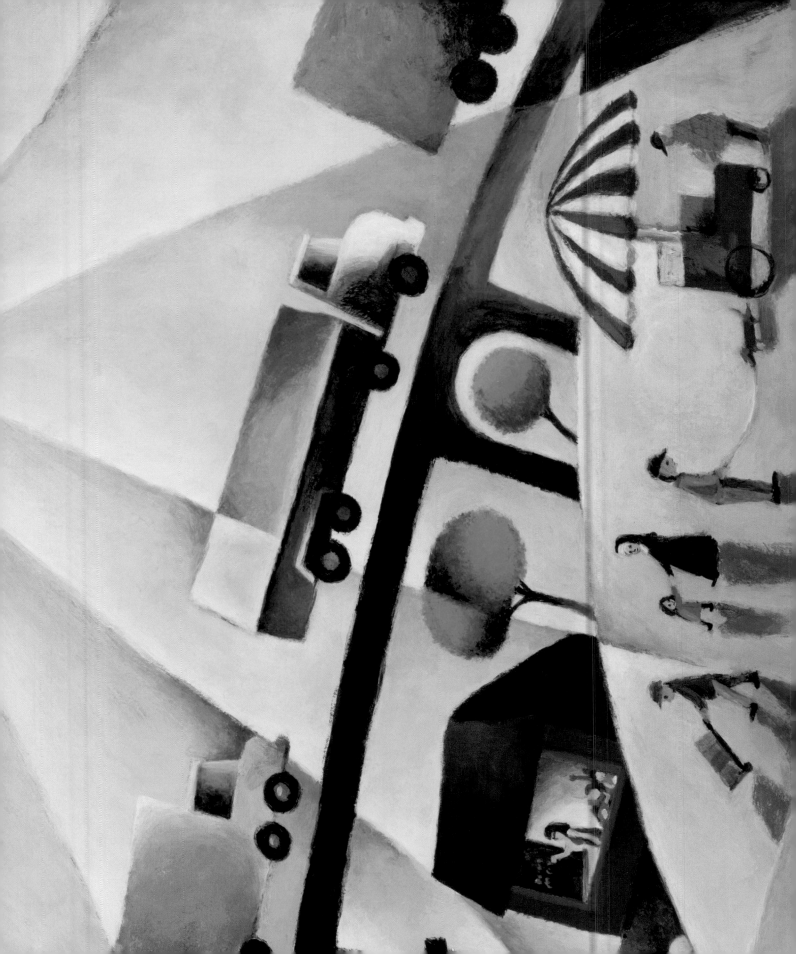

All of us as vital as the one light we move through,

the same light on blackboards with lessons for the day:

equations to solve, history to question, or atoms imagined,

the "I have a dream" we keep dreaming,

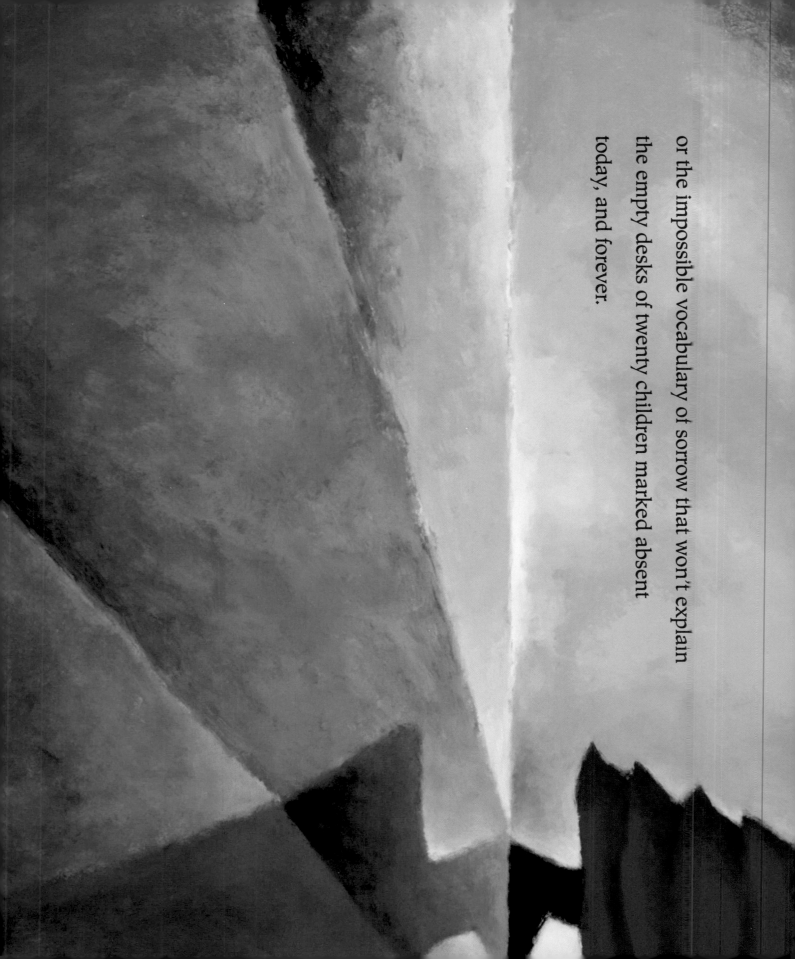

or the impossible vocabulary of sorrow that won't explain
the empty desks of twenty children marked absent
today, and forever.

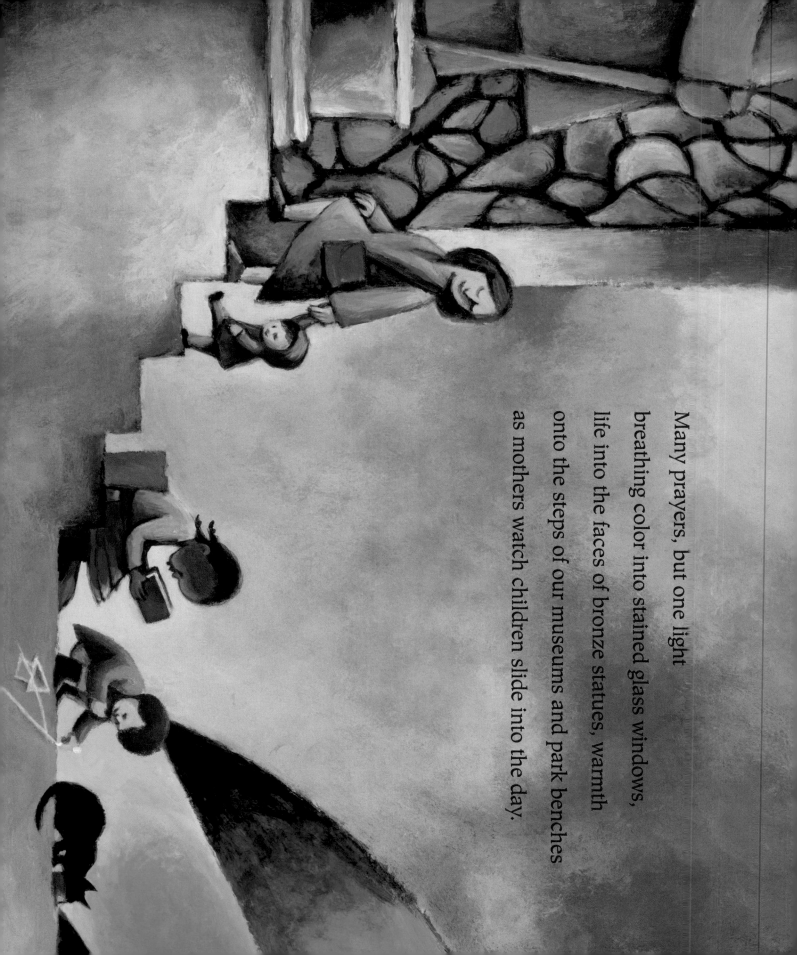

Many prayers, but one light
breathing color into stained glass windows,
life into the faces of bronze statues, warmth
onto the steps of our museums and park benches
as mothers watch children slide into the day.

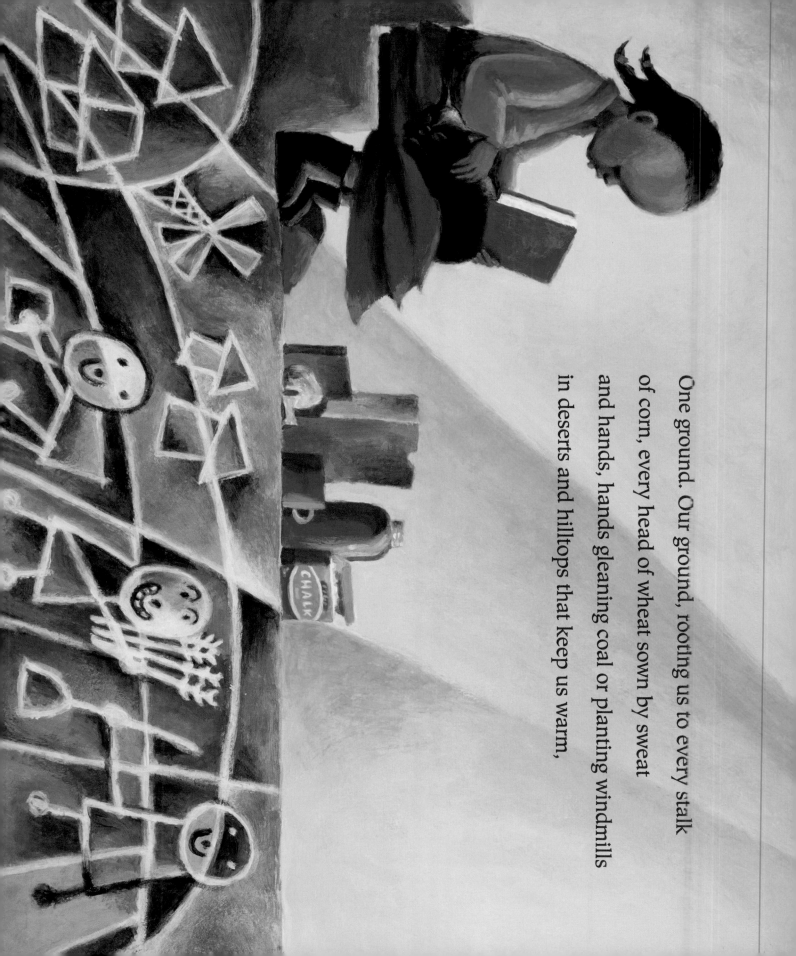

One ground. Our ground, rooting us to every stalk
of corn, every head of wheat sown by sweat
and hands, hands gleaning coal or planting windmills
in deserts and hilltops that keep us warm,

hands digging trenches, routing pipes and cables, hands

as worn as my father's cutting sugarcane

so my brother and I could have books and shoes.

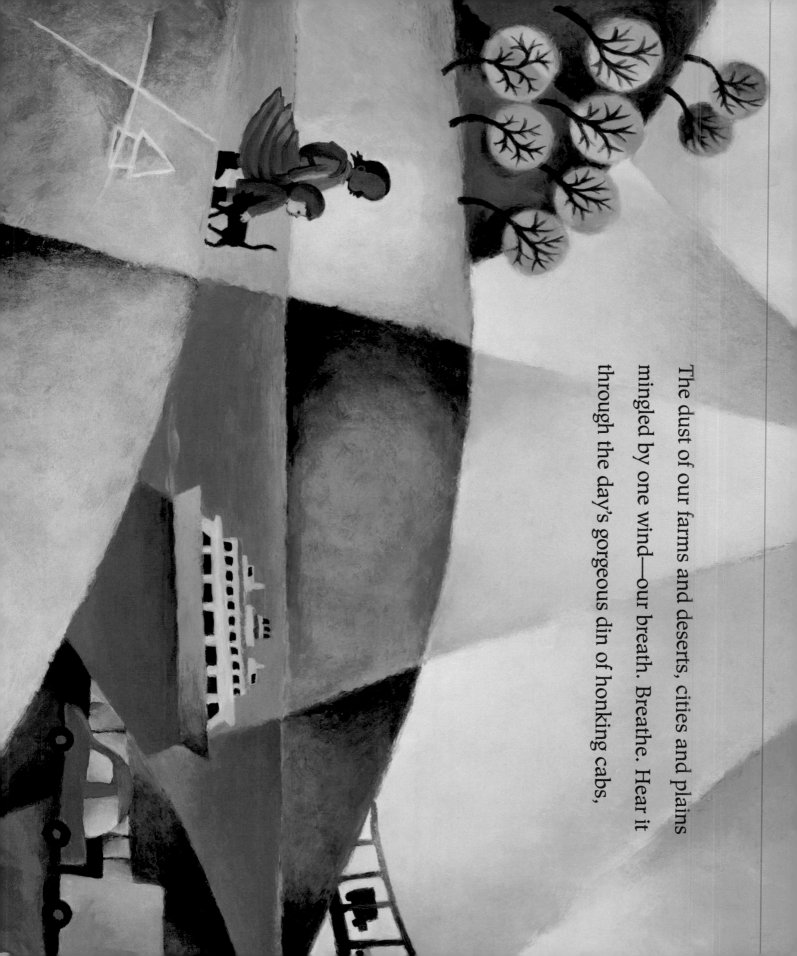

The dust of our farms and deserts, cities and plains
mingled by one wind—our breath. Breathe. Hear it
through the day's gorgeous din of honking cabs,

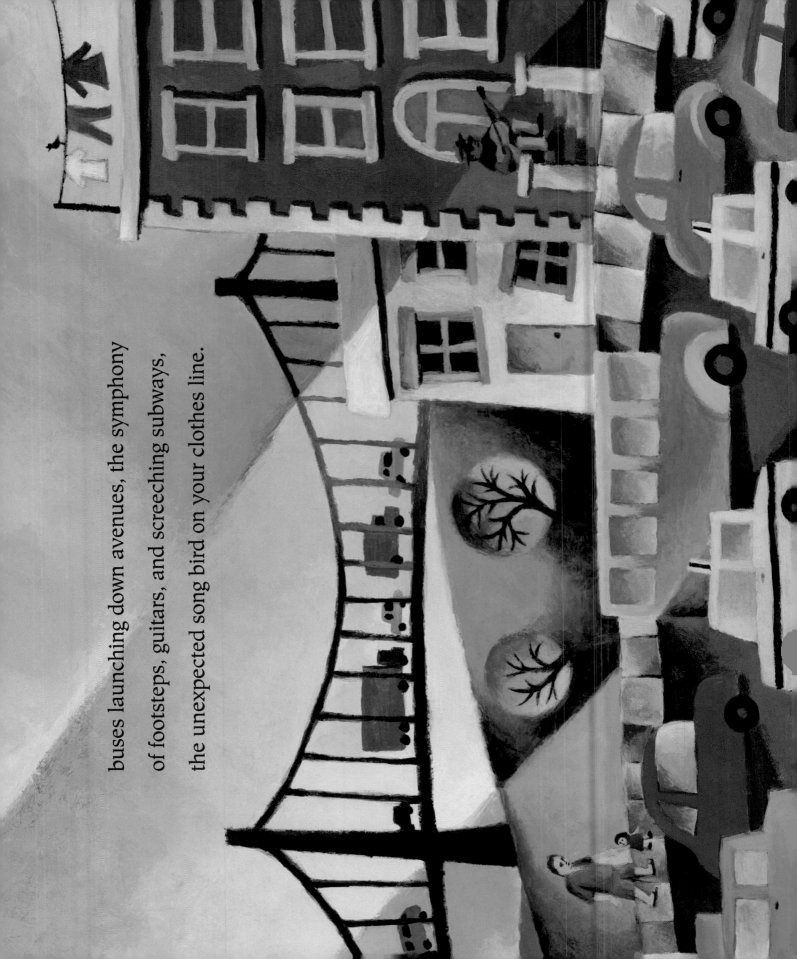

buses launching down avenues, the symphony
of footsteps, guitars, and screeching subways,
the unexpected song bird on your clothes line.

Hear: squeaky playground swings, trains whistling,
or whispers across café tables. Hear: the doors we open
for each other all day, saying: hello / shalom /
buon giorno / howdy / namaste / or buenos días

in the language my mother taught me—in every language

spoken into one wind carrying our lives

without prejudice, as these words break from my lips.

One sky: since the Appalachians and Sierras claimed
their majesty, and the Mississippi and Colorado worked
their way to the sea. Thank the work of our hands:

weaving steel into bridges, finishing one more report

for the boss on time, stitching another wound

or uniform, the first brush stroke on a portrait,

or the last floor on the Freedom Tower

jutting into a sky that yields to our resilience.

One sky, toward which we sometimes lift our eyes
tired from work: some days guessing at the weather
of our lives, some days giving thanks for a love
that loves you back,

sometimes praising a mother

who knew how to give, or forgiving a father

who couldn't give what you wanted.

We head home: through the gloss of rain or weight
of snow, or the plum blush of dusk,

but always—home,
always under one sky, our sky.

And always one moon
like a silent drum tapping
on every rooftop
and every window,
of one country—
all of us—
facing the stars.

Hope—a new constellation
waiting for us to map it,

waiting for us to name it—

together.